A NOTE TO PARENTS

When your children are ready to "step into reading," giving them the right books is as crucial to their development as giving them the right food to eat. **Step into Reading®** books feature exciting stories and information reinforced with lively, colorful illustrations that make learning to read fun, satisfying, and rewarding. We have even taken *extra* steps to keep your child engaged by offering Step into Reading Sticker books, Step into Reading Math books, and Step into Reading Phonics books, in addition to fabulous fiction and nonfiction.

Learning to read, Step by Step:

- **Super Early** books (Preschool–Kindergarten) support pre-reading skills. Parent and child can engage in "see and say" reading using the strong picture cues and the few simple words on each page.
- **Early** books (Preschool–Kindergarten) let emergent readers tackle one or two short sentences of large type per page.
- **Step 1** books (Preschool–Grade 1) have the same easy-to-read type as Early, but with more words per page.
- **Step 2** books (Grades 1–3) offer longer and slightly more difficult text while introducing contractions and clauses. Children are often drawn to our exciting natural science nonfiction titles at this level.
- **Step 3** books (Grades 2–3) present paragraphs, chapters, and fully developed plot lines in fiction and nonfiction.
- **Step 4** books (Grades 2–4) feature thrilling nonfiction illustrated with exciting photographs for independent as well as reluctant readers.

Remember: The grade levels assigned to the six steps are intended only as guides. Some children move through all six steps rapidly; others climb the steps over a period of a few years. Either way, these books will help children "step into reading" for life!

For Geri, my Timothy
—J.L.W.

www.randomhouse.com/kids/disney

Library of Congress Cataloging-in-Publication Data
Weinberg, Jennifer, 1970–
Fly, Dumbo, fly! / by Jennifer Liberts Weinberg.
    p. cm. — (Step into reading. Super early)
SUMMARY: Dumbo the circus elephant is unhappy about his large ears, until he discovers that
he can use them to fly.
ISBN 0-7364-2044-4 (trade) — ISBN 0-7364-8015-3 (lib. bdg.)
[1. Elephants—Fiction. 2. Circus—Fiction. 3. Flight—Fiction.]
I. Title. II. Step into reading. Super early book
PZ7.W436135 Fl 2002   [E]—dc21   2001048697

Printed in the United States of America   October 2002   10 9 8 7 6 5 4 3 2 1

Step into Reading®

Walt Disney's DUMBO

Fly, Dumbo, Fly!

A Super Early Book

By Jennifer Liberts Weinberg

Illustrated by Carlo LoRaso and John Kurtz

Random House 🏠 New York

Peekaboo.

Who are you?

Dumbo!

"Achoo!"

Oh, dear.
Big ears.

A parade!

Oh, dear.

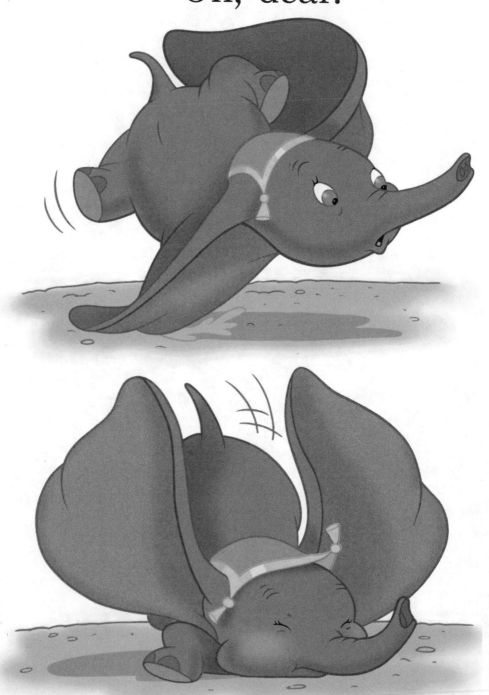

Those ears!

Poor Dumbo.

Who is there?

Timothy Q. Mouse.

"Cheer up, Dumbo!"

Friends!

Dumbo tries.

Dumbo trips!

Wings!

"Jump, Dumbo!"

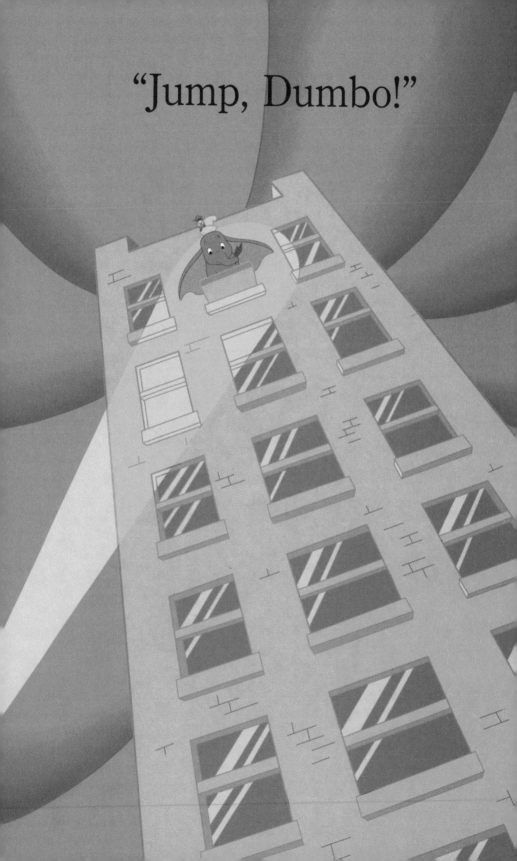

Down, down, down.

"Fly, Dumbo, fly!"
Dumbo tries.

Up, up, up.
Dumbo flies!

Loop-the-loop!

"Way to go, Dumbo!"